MRS. TOGGLE'S BEAUTIFUL BLUE SHOE

Robin Pulver

MRS. TOGGLE'S BEAUTIFUL BLUE SHOE

Illustrated by R. W. Alley

Four Winds Press ⚜ New York
Maxwell Macmillan Canada   Toronto
Maxwell Macmillan International
New York   Oxford   Singapore   Sydney

E
PUL

For Cindy Kane,
who first gave Mrs. Toggle a
chance to kick off

For Bob Alley,
who gave Mrs. Toggle her
beautiful blue shoes

With thanks to Tina Salipante
and Nina Pulver,
for their inspiration and
laughter
—R.P.

For Jennifer Schwarzchild
—R.W.A.

Four Winds Press, Macmillan Publishing Company, 866 Third Avenue, New York, NY 10022
Maxwell Macmillan Canada, Inc., 1200 Eglinton Avenue East, Suite 200, Don Mills, Ontario M3C 3N1
Macmillan Publishing Company is part of the Maxwell Communication Group of Companies.
First edition. Printed and bound in Singapore   10 9 8 7 6 5 4 3 2 1
The text of this book is set in 16 point Berkeley Old Style Book. The illustrations are rendered in watercolor.

Library of Congress Cataloging-in-Publication Data
Pulver, Robin. Mrs. Toggle's beautiful blue shoe / Robin Pulver ; illustrated by R.W. Alley.—1st ed.
p.   cm.
Sequel to: Mrs. Toggle and the dinosaur. c1991.
Summary: Mrs. Toggle joins the children in a game of kickball and loses her beautiful blue shoe.
ISBN 0-02-775456-1
[1. Teachers—Fiction.   2. Schools—Fiction.   3. Humorous stories.]   I. Alley, R. W. (Robert W.), ill.   II. Title.
PZ7.P97325Mqm   1994   [E]—dc20   92-40824

When Mrs. Toggle's students rushed to the playground for recess, Mrs. Toggle stayed at her desk to work. But spring air breezed through the open window. Geese honked in the sky. When she saw the children choosing teams for kickball, Mrs. Toggle hurried to join them.

"Mrs. Toggle!" said Nina. "What are you doing outside?"

"It's spring," replied Mrs. Toggle. "I feel so alive. I couldn't sit still. If you don't mind, I would very much like a turn kicking that ball."

"This is great," said Joey. "Everybody count to three for Mrs. Toggle to kick off."

"One!" yelled the children.

Mrs. Toggle lined herself up with the ball.

"Two!"

Mrs. Toggle got set to kick.

"Three!"

Mrs. Toggle kicked with all her might. Her feet flew out from under her. Mrs. Toggle collapsed, *kerplop*, on the damp spring grass. "How did I do?" she asked.

The children helped her up.

"Um," said Nina. "You missed the ball."
"But you sure kicked off!" said Joey.
"You kicked off your shoe!" explained Paul.
"Uh-oh," said Caroline, pointing.

Mrs. Toggle and the children looked up. High on a tree branch dangled Mrs. Toggle's shoe, blue as the patches of sky that shone through the new spring leaves.

"Oh, my shoe! My beautiful blue shoe!" cried Mrs. Toggle. "How will I ever get it down?"

"Maybe we can knock it down with the ball," said Dina.

"It's worth a try," said Mrs. Toggle.

The children took turns tossing the ball at Mrs. Toggle's shoe. Mrs. Toggle held out her hands to catch it. But the shoe was too high up.

Mrs. Toggle groaned. "Oh, I'm afraid I'll never again have my beautiful blue shoe back on my foot, where it belongs!"

Dina said, "The principal told me to go to him if the answer to a problem ever seems out of reach. Mrs. Toggle's shoe is out of reach."

"We're in luck!" said Joey. "Here comes Mr. Stickler now. He'll know what to do."

The principal frowned as he approached Mrs. Toggle. "Mrs. Toggle," he said, "it's a rule at our school that teachers should set good examples for their students. I was looking out my window, and I saw you with one shoe off and one shoe on. What kind of example is that?"

"I'm sorry, Mr. Stickler," said Mrs. Toggle. "I was overcome by spring."

"She felt so alive," said Dina.

"And couldn't sit still," added Nina.

"She tried to kick the ball, but missed," said Joey.

"She kicked off her shoe instead," pointed out Paul.

"Mrs. Toggle's shoe ended up in that tree," concluded Caroline.

Mr. Stickler stared at Mrs. Toggle's shoe. Finally he said, "Sometimes my cat, Fluffy, gets stuck in a tree when she climbs too high. But there are ways to get her down, if you follow the rules. The first rule is to try calling. Let's call Mrs. Toggle's shoe. Everybody together now…"

"Mr. Stickler!" interrupted Mrs. Toggle. "Shoes are not living things! My shoe cannot move by itself. In my whole life I have never heard of a shoe coming when it's called."

"There's a first time for everything," replied the principal. "All together, children. Call Mrs. Toggle's shoe."

Everybody called, "Shooooe! Shooooe! Mrs. Toggle's shooooe!"

The shoe stayed put.

"I don't think Mrs. Toggle's shoe hears a thing," said Joey.

"A shoe can't hear at all!" explained Paul.

"Still," said Mr. Stickler, "I think we should follow the same rules for getting cats down from trees. If Fluffy doesn't come when I call her, the next thing I try is food. I put Fluffy's favorite food at the bottom of the tree, where she can smell it and see it. Fluffy usually comes down for sardines in olive oil." The principal turned to Mrs. Toggle. "What is your shoe's favorite food?"

"Mr. Stickler!" said Mrs. Toggle. "I don't want to hurt your feelings, but you are being ridiculous. My shoe can't smell, and I have never known it to be hungry."

"There's a first time for everything," said Mr. Stickler. "Why don't you go to the cafeteria? Ask Mrs. Burns to cook up something special for your shoe."

So Mrs. Toggle and the children trooped into the cafeteria. They found the cook, Mrs. Burns, chopping onions for stew.

"Mrs. Burns,"
said Mrs. Toggle,
"Mr. Stickler suggested
that you cook up
something for my shoe."
"Because it's stuck in
a tree," said Joey.
"And won't come down," added Nina.
"Like Mr. Stickler's cat, sometimes,"
explained Caroline.

Mrs. Burns looked at Mrs. Toggle's one bare foot. She pulled
a handkerchief from her pocket and wiped tears from her
eyes. "I get a kick out of you, Mrs. Toggle," she said. "But tell
Mr. Stickler I do not cook special food for shoes. If your shoe
is hungry, it will have to eat what is on the menu for today.
Your shoe must eat stew, like everyone else."

Mrs. Burns washed her hands, then ladled out a bowl of stew for Mrs. Toggle's shoe. "Tell your shoe it can come for…for…more stew!" she said, laughing hard.

On the way back to the playground, Mrs. Toggle said to the children, "I couldn't tell whether Mrs. Burns was laughing or crying about my shoe."

"I think the onions were making her cry," said Caroline.

The children and Mrs. Toggle placed the bowl at the base of the tree. Steam from the stew rose high up to the tree branch where Mrs. Toggle's shoe dangled.

The shoe didn't budge.

"It isn't working," said Mrs. Toggle. "My shoe can't see the stew or smell it."

Mr. Stickler said, "Lots of people's shoes *do* smell, you have to admit. But when calling and food don't work with Fluffy, then I telephone my friends in the fire department. They come with ladders and get her down."

"Hey!" said Joey. "The custodian has a ladder. He uses it when he changes light bulbs. Let's call Mr. Abel."

"Try that if you like," said Mr. Stickler. "Although I can't imagine how changing a light bulb will help Mrs. Toggle's shoe. Meanwhile, I'm going to check on Fluffy. Talking about her makes me miss her."

Joey ran off to find the custodian. Soon he returned with Mr. Abel and the ladder.

"Mr. Abel," said Mrs. Toggle, "I'm so afraid that my beautiful blue shoe will never again be back on my foot, where it belongs."

"Never give up hope," said Mr. Abel, kindly. He propped the ladder against the tree. He extended it to its full length.

"Wow!" said Joey. "I wish I could grow up as fast as that ladder just did!"

Then the children and Mrs. Toggle held the ladder while Mr. Abel climbed up, up, up. He reached Mrs. Toggle's shoe and carried it carefully down to her.

Mrs. Toggle slipped her foot into her beautiful blue shoe. "Oh, Mr. Abel, how can I ever thank you?"

Suddenly, a cat came bounding across the playground, with Mr. Stickler close behind. The cat scrambled right up the tree, high, high into the branches, beyond the reach, even, of Mr. Abel's ladder.

"Uh-oh," said Caroline.

"Don't worry," said Paul. "Mr. Stickler always knows what to do."

As Mrs. Toggle and the children headed back to their classroom they heard the principal calling, "Fluffy! Fluffy!"

"Gee," said Dina, "some people think school is boring!"

"It never is for us," said Joey.

"I know," said Nina. "Isn't it great to be alive?"